For Jake Berube

It's a mouse.
It's a jackass.
It's a
LANE SMITH

ROARING BROOK PRESS
NEW YORK, NEW YORK

What do you
have there?

It's a book.

How do you
scroll down?

I don't.
I turn the page.
It's a book.

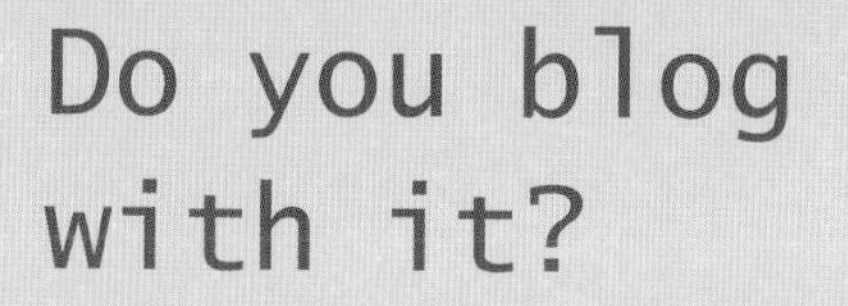

No, it’s a book.

Where's your mouse?

Can you
make the
characters
fight?

Nope.
Book.

Can it text?

No.

Tweet?

No.

Wi-Fi?

No.

Can it do this?

No...

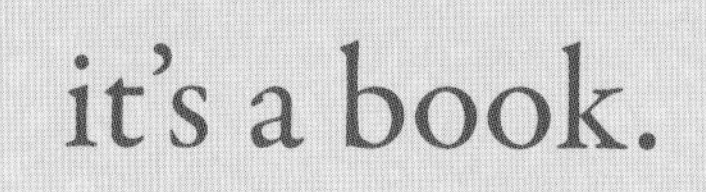

it's a book.

Look.

“Arrrrrrrr,”
nodded Long John Silver,
“we’re in agreement then?”
He unsheathed his broad
cutlass laughing a maniacal
laugh, “Ha! Ha! Ha!”
Jim was petrified.
The end was upon him.
Then in the distance, a ship
A wide smile played across
the lad’s face.

Too many letters.

I'll fix it.

So . . .

what else can this book do?

Does it need
a password?

No.

Need a
screen
name?

It’s a book.

Are you going
to give my
book back?

No.

Fine . . .

I'm going to the library.

Don't worry, I'll charge
it up when I'm done!

You don't have to . . .

IT’S A BOOK, JACKASS.

LANE SMITH wrote a **BOOK** that was a *New York Times* best seller[1]. His illustrations in a **BOOK** won a Caldecott Honor Medal[2]. He wrote and illustrated a **BOOK** that was on many "best book" lists including *School Library Journal*, *The Horn Book*, *Publishers Weekly*, *Parenting* and *Child* magazines, and was a *New York Times* Best Illustrated Book of the Year[3]. He painted the pictures in a **BOOK** that sold millions of copies[4]. He created artwork in a **BOOK** by Roald Dahl and a **BOOK** by Florence Parry Heide and a **BOOK** by Dr. Seuss and Jack Prelutsky[5].

He is married to Molly Leach who designed all of the above **BOOKS**.

[1] *Madam President* [2] *The Stinky Cheese Man and Other Fairly Stupid Tales* written by Jon Scieszka [3] *John, Paul, George & Ben* [4] *The True Story of the Three Little Pigs* written by Jon Scieszka [5] *James and the Giant Peach, Princess Hyacinth (The Surprising Tale of a Girl Who Floated), Hooray for Diffendoofer Day!*

www.lanesmithbooks.com

Published by Roaring Brook Press
Roaring Brook Press is a division of Holtzbrinck Publishing Holdings Limited Partnership
175 Fifth Avenue, New York, New York 10010

www.roaringbrookpress.com

Distributed in Canada by H. B. Fenn and Company Ltd.

Cataloging-in-Publication Data is on file at the Library of Congress
ISBN 978-1-59643-606-0

Roaring Brook Press books are available for special promotions and premiums.
For details contact: Director of Special Markets, Holtzbrinck Publishers.

First Edition August 2010
Book design by Molly Leach
Printed in April 2010 in China by Toppan Leefung Printing Ltd., Dongguan City, Guangdong Province

10 9 8 7 6 5 4 3 2 1